THE STUBBORN
OLD WOMAN

THE STUBBORN OLD WOMAN

By Clyde Robert Bulla

Pictures by Anne Rockwell

THOMAS Y. CROWELL   NEW YORK

Library of Congress Cataloging in Publication Data

Bulla, Clyde Robert. The stubborn old woman.
SUMMARY: An old woman, so stubborn she won't leave her
house and farm which are crumbling into the river, meets
an equally stubborn little girl who wants her to leave.
[1. Obstinacy—Fiction]   I. Rockwell, Anne F.
II. Title.   PZ7.B912Stp   1979   [E]   78-22506
ISBN 0-690-03945-X   ISBN 0-690-03946-8 lib. bdg.

FIRST EDITION

To Ron Pulcini
C. R. B.

To Hannah
A. R.

There was once an old woman who had always had her own way. "I will!" and "I won't!" she would say, and when she had made up her mind, nothing could ever change it.

People would say to her, "You must be the most stubborn woman in the world."

She would nod her head and answer, "That may be true," as if she were a little proud of it.

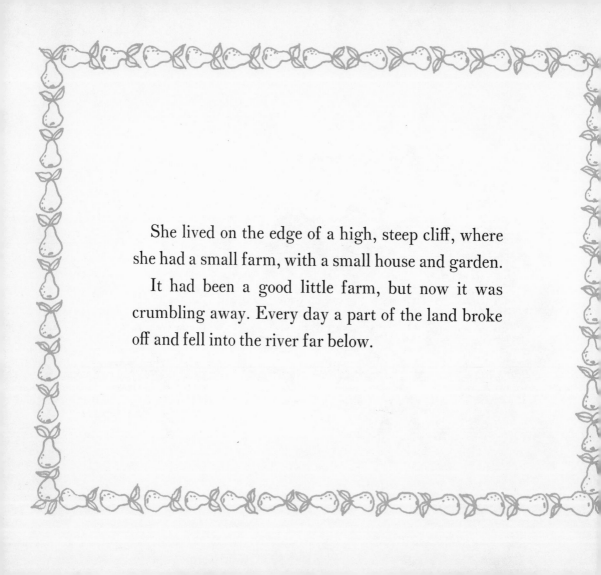

She lived on the edge of a high, steep cliff, where she had a small farm, with a small house and garden.

It had been a good little farm, but now it was crumbling away. Every day a part of the land broke off and fell into the river far below.

The old woman had neighbors—a farmer, a shepherd, and a miller. They came to see her, one at a time. And then they all came together.

"We must talk to you," said the farmer.

"About the same thing, no doubt," said the old woman.

"Yes," said the shepherd.

"Then I won't listen," said the old woman.

"You *must* listen," said the miller. "You cannot stay here any longer."

"All I have is here," said the old woman. "If the river takes my house and garden, let it take me, too."

The neighbors groaned and shook their heads. They went away saying to one another, "Truly she *is* the most stubborn woman in the world!"

Not long afterward a little girl came to the old woman's house.

"I am from the other side of the river," she said. "I live with my brothers and sisters. There are nine of us, and we are orphans."

"Why do you tell *me* this?" asked the old woman.

"We need someone to help look after us," said the little girl. "Someone to sing to us and tell us stories and perhaps bake a birthday cake now and then. Will you come home with me?"

"Did my neighbors send you here?" asked the old woman.

The little girl did not deny it. "We live in a big house," she said. "You would have a room of your own."

"Good day," said the old woman, and she tried to shut the door.

But the little girl had her foot in the doorway. "My home is a day's journey from here, and the sun will soon be down. Please let me stay the night."

"Very well," said the old woman.

In the morning the little girl talked and sang about the house until the old woman told her to go.

"Half the day is gone," said the little girl. "I could not get home before dark."

"And who is to blame for that?" said the old woman. "Stay another night, if you must, but no longer."

"Thank you," said the little girl, "and while I am here, let me tell you more about our home. We have pigs and chickens and a cow. We have two grape vines and a pear tree. It's lovely there, and it will be a place for you to go when you leave this house."

"I won't be leaving this house," said the old woman, "and the sooner you find it out, the better."

Early the next morning she woke the little girl and put her out the front door.

The little girl came in the back door. "You may as well know," she said, "I'll not go until you do."

"I think you will," said the old woman.

"No," said the little girl.

"I really think you will," said the old woman, and she sang very softly:

> *"If beneath my roof you sleep,*
> *You must work to earn your keep."*

She set the little girl to one task after another. "Sweep the house," she said. "Wash the windows . . . Scrub the floor . . . Wash the clothes."

The little girl did everything she was told. Every night she said, "The time is short. Are you going with me now?"

"You know my answer," said the old woman.

And so eleven days passed.

On the morning of the twelfth day the little girl said, "There's no time left. All night I heard the land crumbling away."

"Then go," said the old woman.

"Are you ready to go with me?"

"You know my answer," said the old woman, and she sang again:

> "If beneath my roof you sleep,
> You must work to earn your keep."

"What shall I do?" asked the little girl.

The old woman could find no more work to be done in the house. "Weed the garden," she said.

The little girl went out.

An hour went by, and another. The little girl had not come in. The old woman looked out. Only half the garden was there. While she looked, the other half crumbled and fell into the river far below.

The little girl was gone.

"Where are you?" called the old woman.

There was no answer.

"Little girl—little girl!" called the old woman.

Still there was no answer.

The old woman ran up the road to the farmer's house. "The little girl is gone!" she cried.

"Where?" asked the farmer.

"I sent her to weed the garden," said the old woman. "Now the garden is gone, and the little girl with it. What shall I do?"

"What *can* you do except be sorry?" said the farmer.

She ran to the shepherd's house. "My garden is gone, and the little girl with it. If only I hadn't sent her there! What shall I do?"

"Nothing except take the blame," said the shepherd.

She ran on to the mill. "My garden is gone, and the little girl with it. I sent her there, so I'm to blame. Oh, what shall I do?"

"What *is* there to do but cry and tear your hair?" said the miller.

"Oh, I *will* cry and tear my hair," said the old woman. "I'll be sorry all the rest of my days, and I'll go through the world telling everyone what a wicked old woman I am!"

She went down the road, weeping and tearing her hair.

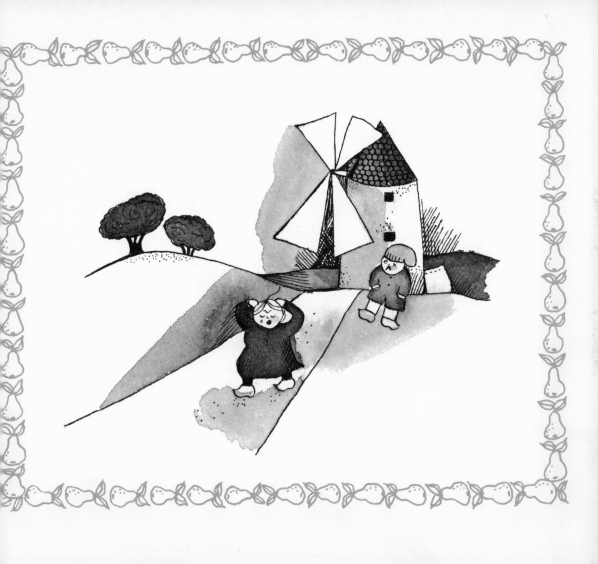

As night fell she sat on a stone to rest. Someone came up beside her. A voice said, "Old woman, I bring you news, both bad and good."

"Go quickly by," she said, "for there's no one wickeder than I. Once there was a little girl, and now she's gone because of me."

"Listen," said the voice, "your house has fallen into the river. That is the bad news. But here is the good. No one was in it when it fell."

"It matters not," said the old woman. "My garden is in the river, too, and the little girl with it, and I'm to blame. Such a good little girl she was—so cheerful about the house. The best little girl in the world, except for being so stubborn." Then she cried louder. "No, it's I who was stubborn. I wouldn't listen, and now the little girl is gone!"

"Stop crying," said the voice. "Put the hair out of your eyes and look at me."

She pushed back her hair, and there before her was the little girl.

"Oh, mercy!" The old woman fell into the dirt. "It's a ghost come to haunt me!"

"Get up," said the little girl. "I'm not a ghost."

"You're not?" The old woman sat up and looked at her. "Then how did you get here?"

"You sent me to the garden," said the little girl, "but it was crumbling away, so I didn't go. Instead I hid in the bushes across the road."

"You did?"

"Yes. I thought you might come looking for me."

"Did you hear me call?"

"Yes," said the little girl.

"But you didn't answer."

"No," said the little girl.

"That was wicked," said the old woman.

"But you did come looking for me," said the little girl, "and that brought you out of the house."

Now the old woman was laughing and crying. "What a wise little girl you are! Far wiser than I. But I will be better. And one day I'll build another house, and you shall live with me."

"While we wait," said the little girl, "why don't you come home with me? You may like it there."

So they walked all night and came to the little girl's house at sunrise. All her brothers and sisters ran out to meet them and give them a cheer.

The old woman found that she did like it there. She settled down to looking after the orphans. She sang them songs and told them stories and baked cakes on their birthdays, and she was hardly ever stubborn again.